NO AR

D1298012

New House

Story by Joyce Maynard

Pictures by Steve Bethel

Ro 32498

HARCOURT BRACE JOVANOVICH, PUBLISHERS

San Diego   New York   London

For Sheri and Mode

Text copyright © 1987 by Joyce Maynard
Illustrations copyright © 1987 by Steve Bethel

All rights reserved.
No part of this publication may be reproduced or transmitted in any form
or by any means, electronic or mechanical, including photocopy, recording,
or any information storage and retrieval system, without permission
in writing from the publisher.

Requests for permission to make copies of any part of the work should be mailed to:
Permissions, Harcourt Brace Jovanovich, Publishers, Orlando, Florida 32887.

Library of Congress Cataloging-in-Publication Data

Maynard, Joyce, 1953–
New house.

Summary: Andy uses the scrap material from the new house
going up down the street to build a tree house.
[1. Building—Fiction. 2. Tree houses—Fiction]
I. Bethel, Steve, ill. II. Title.
PZ7.M4716Ne   1987   [E]   86-4820
ISBN 0-15-257042-X

Printed in the United States of America
First edition
A B C D E

The paintings in this book were done in acrylic on Monadnock paper.

The text type was set in ITC Century Book by Central Graphics, San Diego, California.

The display type was set in Bookman Contour by Thompson Type, San Diego, California.

Printed and bound by Tien Wah Press, Singapore

Production supervision by Warren Wallerstein and Eileen McGlone

Designed by Michael Farmer

Andy's house was the only one at the end of a long dirt road. Now that it was summer, Andy spent a lot of time riding his bike up and down the road and throwing sticks for his dog, Bud. Sometimes he climbed the big maple tree in front of the house.

One day a blue truck parked on Andy's road, and a couple of men got out. The men put orange ribbons on some of the trees. Then they drove away.

That night at dinner, Andy told his mom and dad about the men.

"Maybe somebody bought the Donovans' land," said Mom. "Who knows? Maybe we'll get some neighbors."

"And maybe there'll be somebody my age," said Andy.

The next day he watched for the blue truck, but it never came. It didn't come back the next day, or the day after that.

One morning when Andy was eating his cereal he heard Bud barking, and a rumbling noise getting closer and closer. He ran outside and saw a huge skidder driving into the woods. A man with a roaring chain saw was already at work. Every few minutes a tree came down.

Crraack. The tree broke at the base. *Craashh.* The branches swept to the ground. The trunk hit. *Boom.*

Andy felt the ground tremble. The skidder rumbled back and forth, pushing branches into one pile, dragging trunks into another.

A man watched from the road. "My name is Red," he told Andy. "I'm putting up a house here. These guys are clearing the lot for me."

"Are you going to be our neighbor?" Andy asked.

"It won't be my house," said Red. "I'm the builder. A family will probably buy the house, but I don't know who."

By the end of the afternoon, there was a big sunny patch where the woods used to be. Andy came back to see the log truck loading up the pile of trunks with its cherry picker.

A couple of days later when Andy was still in bed, he heard the rumbling noise again. It was a bulldozer this time, and a backhoe. Red showed the men where to dig the cellar hole. They worked late into the afternoon.

After they were gone, Andy rode his bike up and down the dirt piles and in and out of the cellar hole until he had worn paths in the dirt.

Over the next week, men and trucks came and went, spreading crushed stone and laying drainage pipes.

Then came the cement mixer. The barrel turned. The man pulled the lever and concrete sloshed and slid down the chute. It filled up plywood forms like batter poured into a pan.

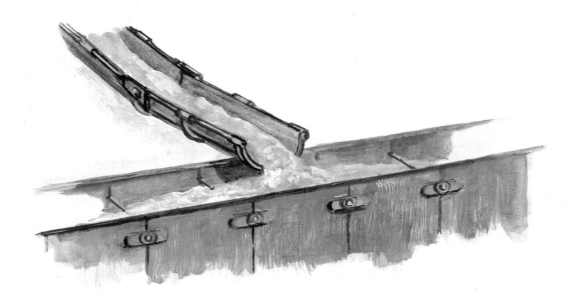

The next day the men took the plywood off. There it stood: a perfect concrete box with one wide door.

After the trucks and men had left, Andy went up for a closer look. He touched the walls—lightly at first, in case they were still wet. But they were hard. Andy saw lines in the walls where the forms had joined together, and smaller lines, like fingerprints, left by the grain of the plywood. He walked inside the box where it was quiet, and yelled like Tarzan.

Red was back, with a tool belt and nail apron and two other carpenters. The men kept talking about "2 by 4's" and "2 by 6's" as they unloaded the lumber truck. Red was very busy. He barely gave Andy a nod. The men set up sawhorses and started measuring and cutting, throwing their scraps into a pile. They set joists on the foundation, in a row, and nailed them to the sill. *Pow pow pow.* And another one. *Pow pow pow.*

Suddenly the racket stopped, and the men sat down with their lunch pails for a break. Andy joined them.

"This is John and this is Gary. They work with me," said Red.

"You guys work hard," said Andy.

The men laughed. "That's what we're paid for," said John.

"I was wondering what you're going to do with the scrap wood," said Andy.

"You can have it," said Red. "Help yourself to any bent or dropped nails you find too."

Andy ran back home to get his wagon. He hauled the scrap wood over to his climbing tree. "I know just what to build," he told Bud.

The next day the carpenters laid out sheets of plywood over the floor joists and nailed them down to make a platform.

Over in his yard, Andy used his dad's hammer to nail five pieces of wood onto the trunk of the big maple, like rungs of a ladder. Then he climbed up to where the branches spread. He could see all the way to where his mailbox stood.

He tried nailing some 2 by 6's across the tree branches to make a floor. But some branches were too high, and some wood was too short. One of Andy's nails hit a knot in a board and bent, and he dropped his hammer. He felt like crying.

"Dumb tree," he said.

"Hey, what kind of talk is that?" called Red. "Everybody makes mistakes. Let me give you some pointers."

By Monday morning Andy had a platform to sit on. He ate a granola bar and watched Red and John and Gary start to saw a stack of 2 by 6's. They built a whole wall, flat on the deck, leaving spaces for five windows and a door. When the wall was done the men slowly raised it and propped it in place. Then they started on the next wall.

Over at the maple, Andy sawed 2 by 4's, all the same length, and lifted them with a rope, one at a time, into the tree. He nailed them together to make a big square for a wall. After lunch he raised the wall so it leaned against a branch. Then he nailed it in place. "I can't believe I did that," he said.

Every morning now, Andy put on his work clothes and packed his school lunchbox with a sandwich and a thermos of milk. When Red and his men took a break for lunch, Andy joined them, usually with his wagon so he could get another load of scraps. While they munched on cookies, Red explained how to make triangle-shaped trusses to hold up the roof.

"A triangle is the strongest shape," said Red.

"Want to come up and see my tree house?" Andy asked.

"I might break the floorboards," said Red. "You'd better find someone closer to your size."

After the trusses were in place, the men covered the walls with plywood and cut out the doors and windows. At lunch that day Andy asked about the scraps from the windows.

"Tell me what size your walls are and I'll trim the scraps so they fit," said Gary. "I'll show you how to use a tape measure to get the sizes right."

Andy used Gary's tape to measure the roof and walls. Then he drew all the shapes and wrote the measurements he needed on a piece of paper.

"This won't take long," said Gary, snapping chalk lines on the boards and buzzing through the lines with his circular saw. Andy had to hurry to keep up, loading the pieces on his wagon.

Summer was half over. As the days passed, Andy worked on his tree house, and kept his eye on the action next door:

An electrician ran wires all through Red's house. Plumbers routed pipes through the floor and walls to carry hot and cold water to faucets. A truck delivered two toilets, one white and one blue, and three sinks and a bathtub. Insulators wearing masks over their mouths and noses unrolled lengths of pink fluffy fiberglass and stapled them between the studs. A mason started working in the basement with cinder blocks and mortar, building up the chimney. When he got as high as the living room floor, he cut out a hole and kept going.

Now the house reminded Andy of a display at the science museum where you look inside a man's skin and see all his bones and veins and muscles.

In a few days, Dave and Steve, the sheetrockers, had put up the ceilings and walls with their screwguns. By the end of the week they were up on stilts smoothing plaster onto the ceiling.

"You two guys could be in the circus," said Andy.

Just then Red walked in, smiling. "It's sold," he said. "This house is sold. The family moves in at the end of the summer. There are two kids, Andy, but I don't know how old they are."

As Red and Andy walked through the rooms, Andy figured out where the kitchen would be, and the dining room, the living room, and the two bathrooms. Andy could look out the window of one bedroom and see his tree house. If a friend lived here, they could send messages back and forth with mirrors or walkie-talkies, or maybe even set up a pulley between their two houses.

Andy's tree house was almost finished now too. He pieced together wood scraps to cover the roof like patches on a quilt. For a spyglass he hung a length of plastic pipe the plumbers left behind.

Then he went on vacation with his parents for two weeks, up to the lake.

As they drove home past the new house, Andy asked to get out so he could see what Red and Gary and John had been up to.

The garage door was on. Half the clapboards were painted. The chimney stuck out through the roof.

He looked in the window. There was carpet covering the plywood floors. The ceilings were smooth and white. The walls in each room were painted a different color. There was trim around the windows and the doors between the rooms, and cabinets in the kitchen. The house smelled of varnish and fresh paint.

A few days passed. As the painters put the finishing touches on the new house, Andy went up in the tree house, same as always, to hammer in a few last boards.

He heard Red, calling up to him. "I stopped over to say good-bye," he said. "And I thought you might want this paint left over from the kitchen."

Red eyed the tree house for a minute. "You did a fine job on this place," he said.

"Someday I want to be a builder like you," said Andy.

"You'll be a good one," said Red.

After Red left, Andy put on an old shirt and borrowed a brush from his dad, and started painting. When he was nearly done, he looked out the window and saw a moving van back into the driveway of the new house. Men unloaded boxes and boxes, couches, chairs, mattresses, and a big round table, and carried them into the house. They unloaded a red tricycle and a dirt bike just like Andy's.

Just then a car pulled in. A man got out first. Then a woman and a little girl. Then a boy Andy's size.

Andy put the lid on the paint and climbed down his ladder. He rode his bike over to the new house and laid it in the dirt. "Is this your new house?" he asked the boy.

"Yup. I'm Peter," said the boy. "Is that your tree house?"

"Yeah, do you want to come see it?" said Andy.

"You bet."

Gorham MacBane Public Library

3GRM000939

05

GORHAM MACBANE PUBLIC LIBRARY
SPRINGFIELD, TENNESSEE

OCT 1 9 1999

NOV 0 2 1999

NOV 1 2 1999

NOV 2 9 1999

JUL 0 8 2000

JUL 2 1 2000

OCT 3 1 2000

APR 3 0 2001

JUN 2 8 2001

JUL 1 6 2001

OCT 1 0 2001

APR 0 6 2002

APR 1 9 2002

OCT 0 6 1999